This bo

Published by Ladybird Books Ltd .
80 Strand London WC2R 0RL
A Penguin Company

17 19 20 18

Printed in Italy

Hansel
and
Gretel

illustrated by Claire Pound

Ladybird

Hansel and Gretel lived with
their father and stepmother
in a little house near a wood.

Their father was a woodcutter,
and he was very poor.

They were all very hungry.

One day Hansel and Gretel's father said, "We have no money left. There is no more food for us to eat."

"Then Hansel and Gretel cannot live here," said their stepmother. "We must leave them in the middle of the wood."

"No," said their father.

But their stepmother said, "We must."

Hansel and Gretel were
listening at the door.

"I have a plan," said Hansel,
and he went out to get
some pebbles.

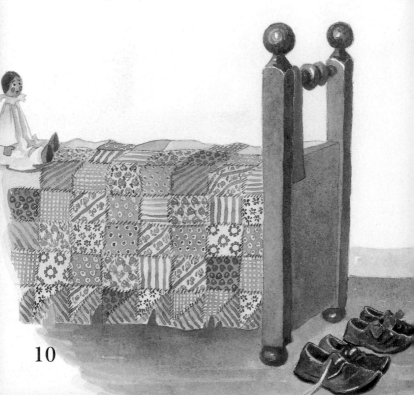

11

The next day they all went into the wood.

Hansel dropped pebbles on the path.

"Wait here," said their father.
"We are going to collect wood."

Hansel and Gretel waited all
day. Then they followed the
pebbles back home.

The woodcutter was glad to see Hansel and Gretel, but their stepmother was angry.

"There is not enough food for us all," she said. "We must take Hansel and Gretel deeper into the wood."

"No!" said their father. "We can't do that."

"We must," said their stepmother. "This time they must not find their way home."

Hansel's stepmother locked the door so that Hansel couldn't get out. He couldn't collect pebbles.

21

The next day they all went deep into the wood. This time Hansel dropped breadcrumbs on the path.

"Wait here," said their father. "We are going to collect wood."

Hansel and Gretel waited all day. Then they looked for the breadcrumbs on the path. But the birds had eaten all the breadcrumbs.

Hansel and Gretel went deeper into the wood. They walked for a long time.

In the middle of the wood, they found a house made of sweets and cakes.

In the house lived a witch.
The witch planned to eat
Hansel and Gretel.

She locked Hansel in a cage
and gave him lots of food.

"Soon he will be fat enough to eat," said the witch. "Then I will cook him in my fire."

"Where is the fire?" said Gretel.

"Here," said the witch. And she opened the oven door.

"I can't see the fire," said Gretel.

The witch opened the oven door a little wider.

"I still can't see it," said Gretel.

The witch opened the oven door as wide as she could.

Gretel pushed her in and locked the door.

Gretel let Hansel out of the cage.

"Look at all this money," said Gretel. "We can take this home and buy food with it."

After a long walk Hansel
and Gretel found their
way home.

Their father was very glad to
see them.

"Your stepmother has gone,"
he said.

So Hansel and Gretel and their father all lived happily ever after in their little house near the wood.

Read It Yourself is a series of graded readers designed to give young children a confident and successful start to reading.

Level 3 is suitable for children who are developing reading confidence and stamina, and who are ready to progress to longer stories with a wider vocabulary. The stories are told simply and with a richness of language.

About this book

At this stage of reading development, it's rewarding to ask children how they prefer to approach each new story. Some children like to look first at the pictures and discuss them with an adult. Some children prefer the adult to read the story to them before they attempt it for themselves. Many children at this stage will be eager to read the story aloud to an adult at once, and to discuss it afterwards. Unknown words can be worked out by looking at the beginning letter (*what sound does this letter make?*) and the sounds the child recognises within the word. The child can then decide which word would make sense.

Developing readers need lots of praise and encouragement.